10/03

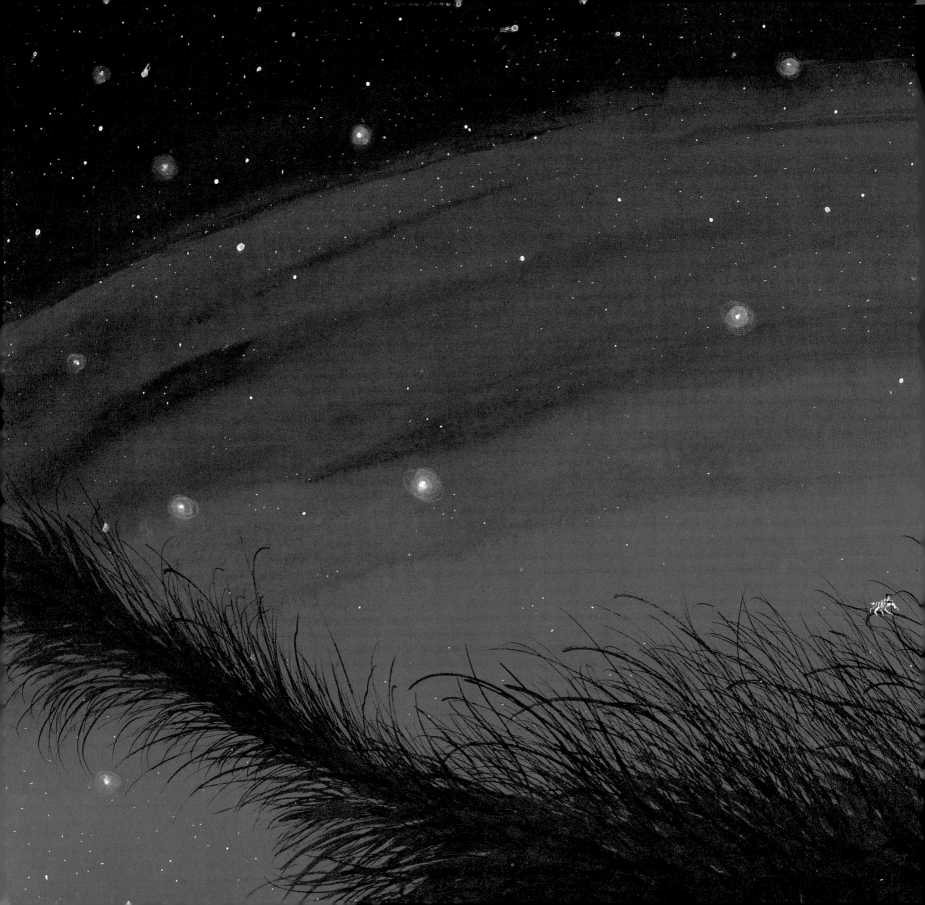

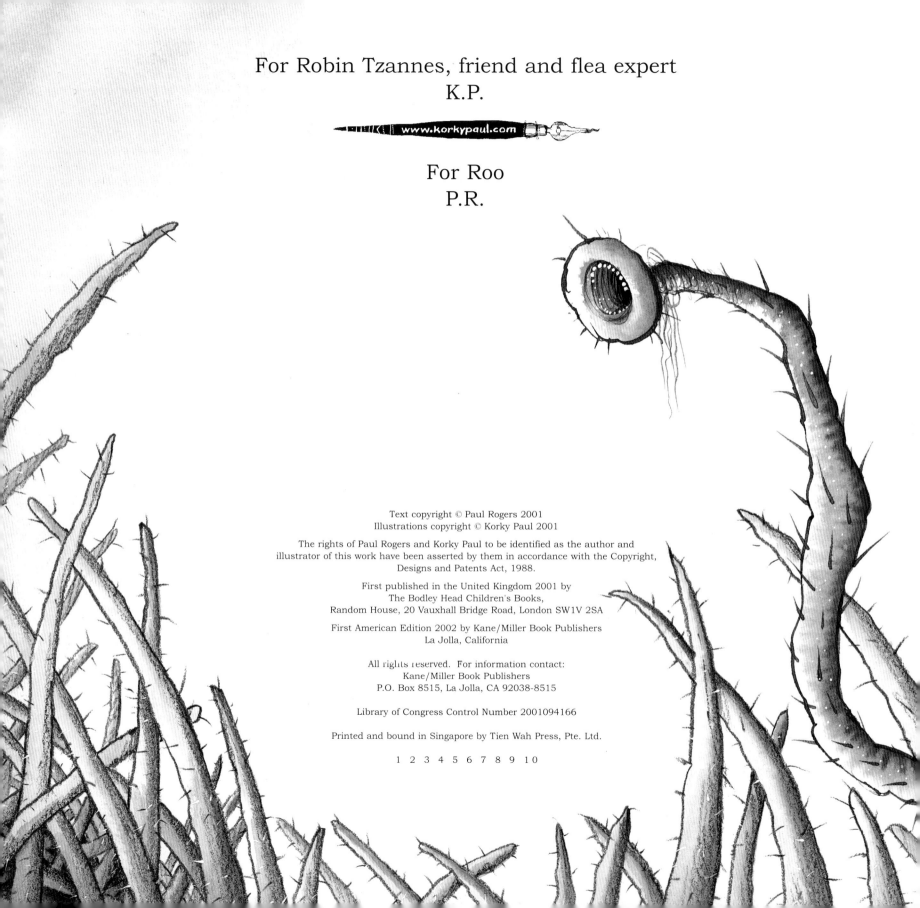

For Robin Tzannes, friend and flea expert
K.P.

www.korkypaul.com

For Roo
P.R.

Text copyright © Paul Rogers 2001
Illustrations copyright © Korky Paul 2001

The rights of Paul Rogers and Korky Paul to be identified as the author and
illustrator of this work have been asserted by them in accordance with the Copyright,
Designs and Patents Act, 1988.

First published in the United Kingdom 2001 by
The Bodley Head Children's Books,
Random House, 20 Vauxhall Bridge Road, London SW1V 2SA

First American Edition 2002 by Kane/Miller Book Publishers
La Jolla, California

All rights reserved. For information contact:
Kane/Miller Book Publishers
P.O. Box 8515, La Jolla, CA 92038-8515

Library of Congress Control Number 2001094166

Printed and bound in Singapore by Tien Wah Press, Pte. Ltd.

1 2 3 4 5 6 7 8 9 10

Paul Rogers & Korky Paul

Tiny

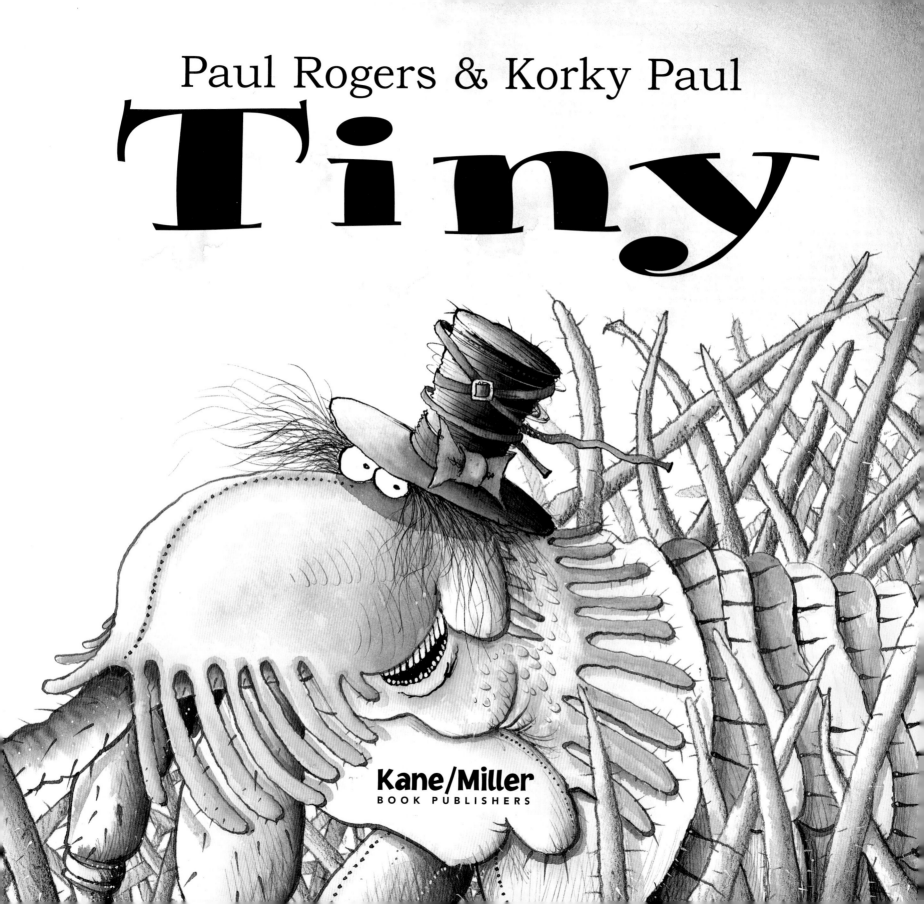

Kane/Miller
BOOK PUBLISHERS

Once upon a time there was a flea called Tiny.

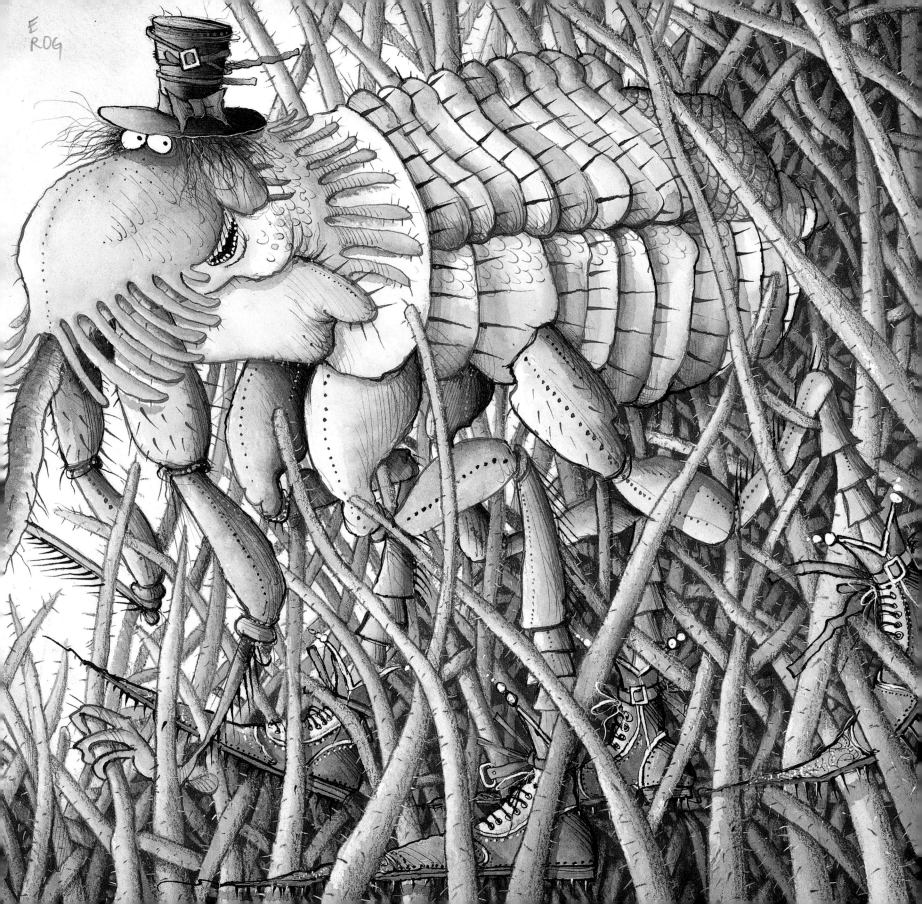

called Cleopatra.

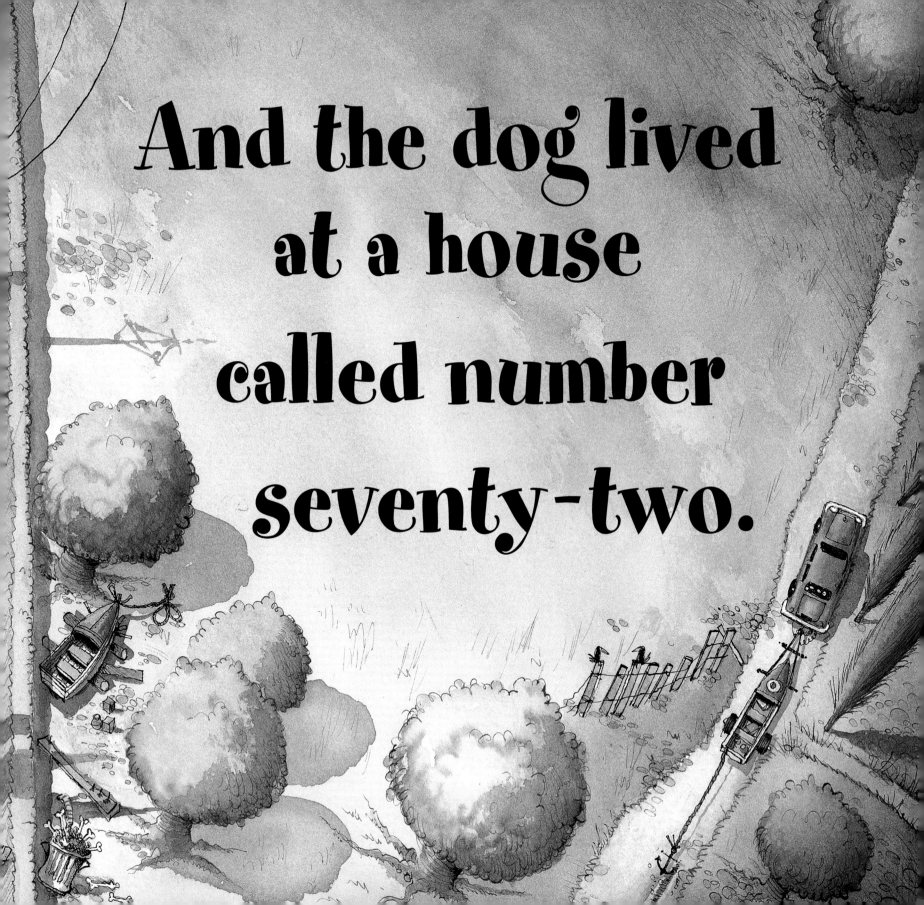

And the dog lived
at a house
called number
seventy-two.

And the house was
in a road

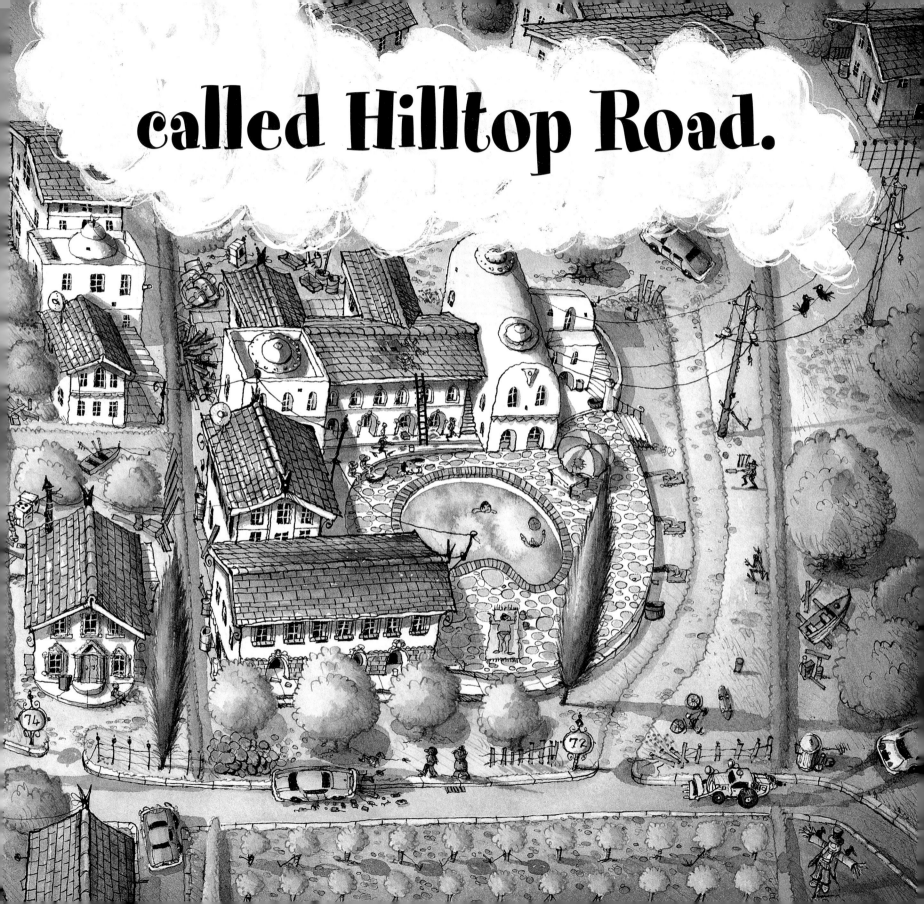

called Hilltop Road.

And the road was in a town

called Remembrance.

And the town was on an island

called Great Hope.

And the island was in the ocean on a planet

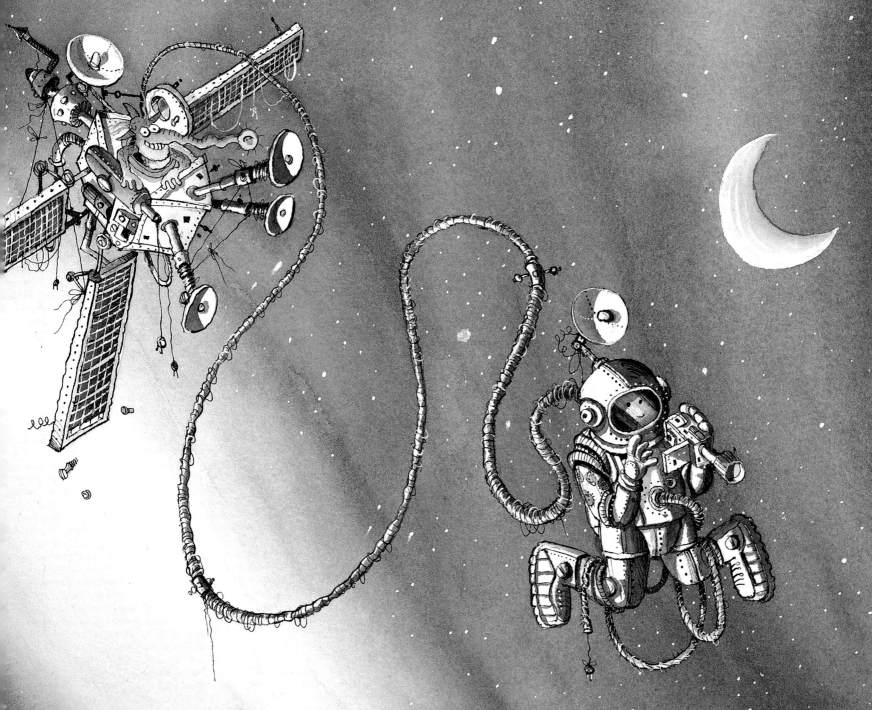

called Earth.

And the Earth was in a sort of heavenly merry-go-round

And the solar system was in a galaxy

full of huge stars far bigger than the sun.

And one evening Cleopatra had a jolly good scratch and Tiny fell off and landed on his back.

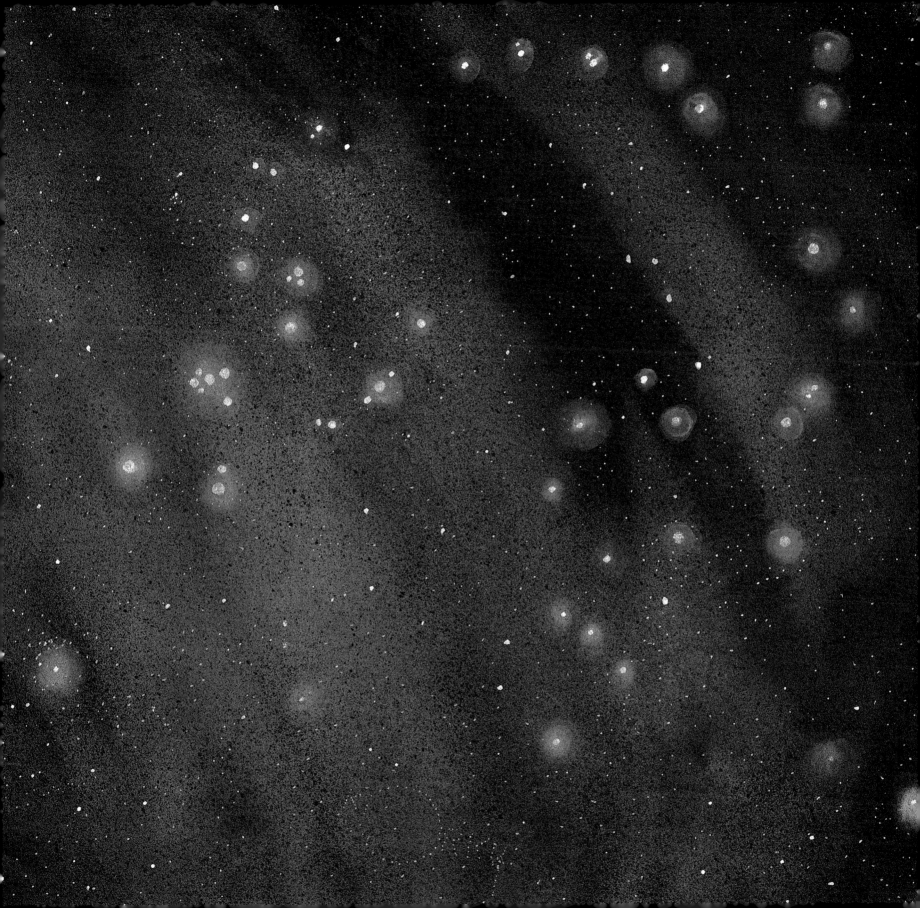

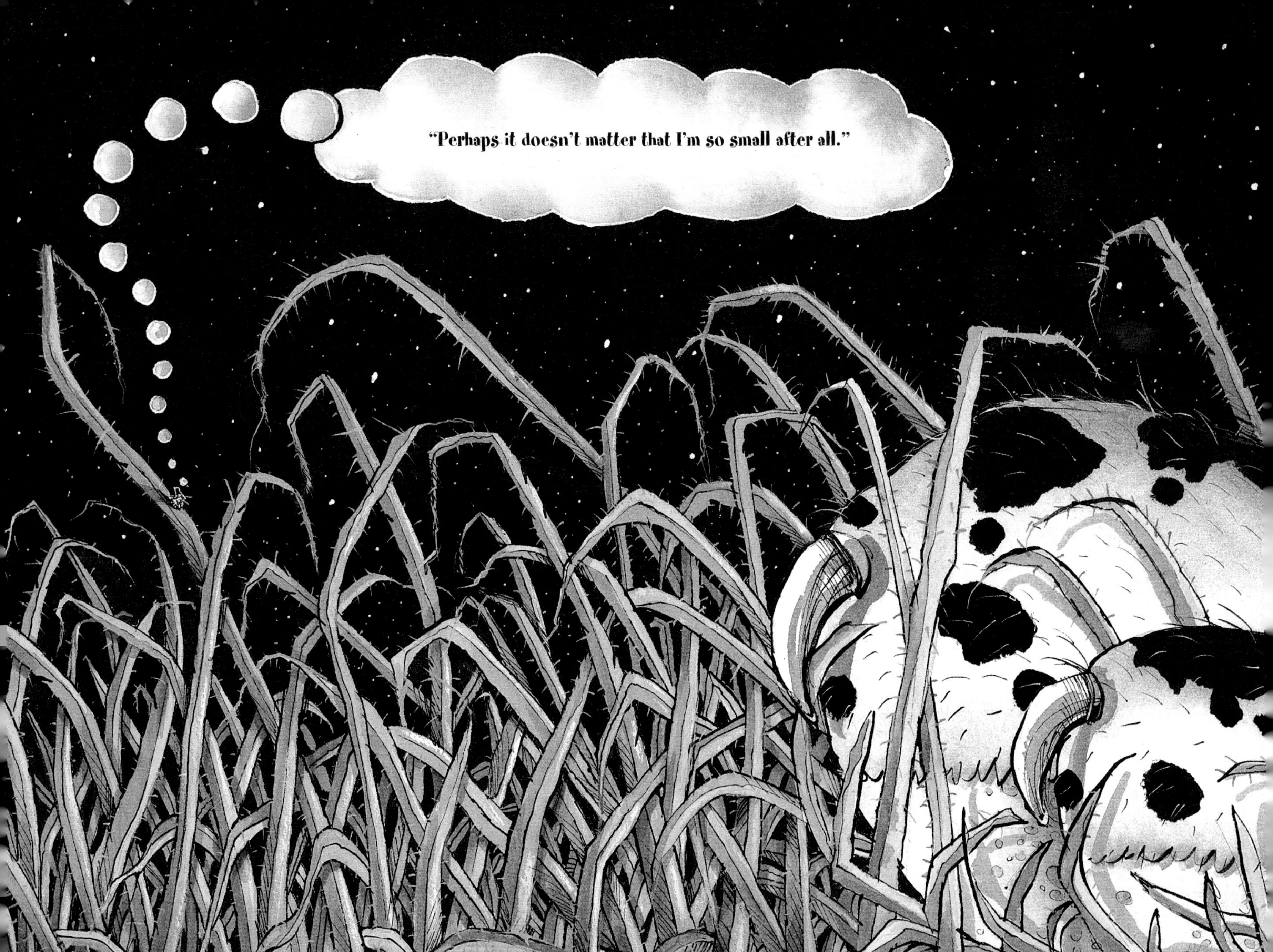

And thinking that happy thought, he sat there waiting...

...until the next dog came along.

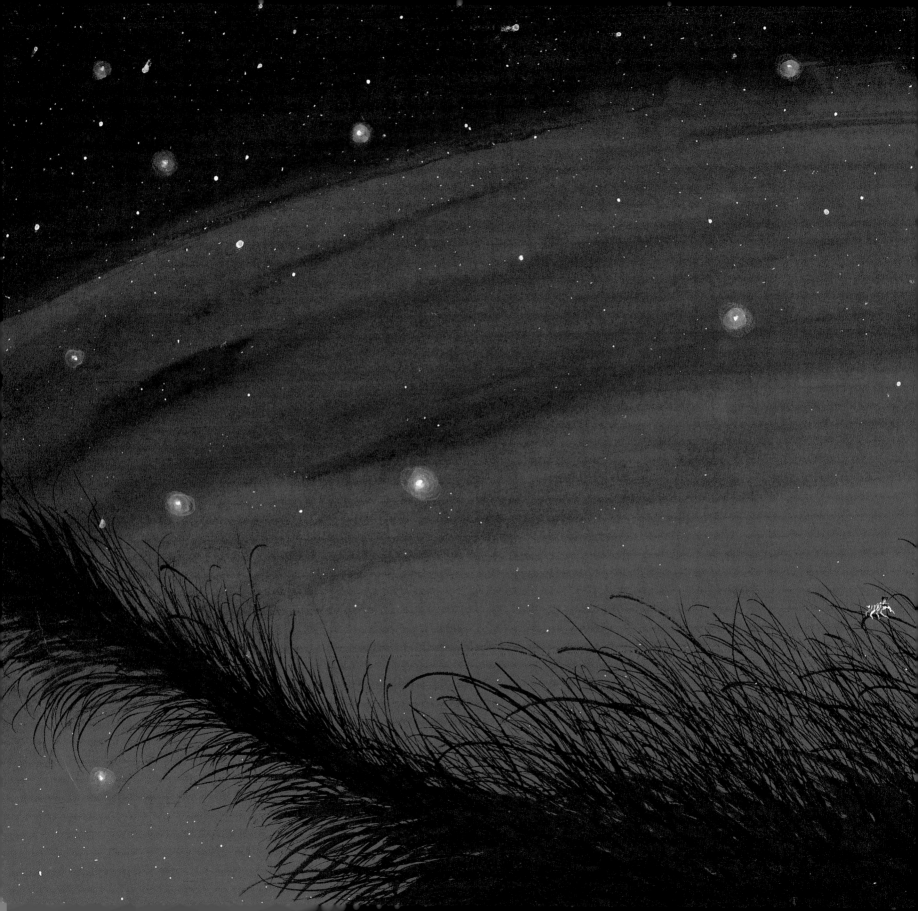